FREAKY
PHENOMENA

CONSCIOUSNESS

FREAKY PHENOMENA

The Series

CONSCIOUSNESS

FAITH

HEALING

LIFE AFTER DEATH

MYSTERIOUS PLACES

PERSONALITY

PSYCHIC ABILITIES

THE SENSES

FREAKY PHENOMENA

CONSCIOUSNESS

Don Rauf

Foreword by Joe Nickell, Senior Research Fellow, Committee for Skeptical Inquiry

MASON CREST

Mason Crest
450 Parkway Drive, Suite D Broomall, PA 19008
www.masoncrest.com

Printed in the United States of America

First printing
9 8 7 6 5 4 3 2 1

Series ISBN: 978-1-4222-3772-4
Hardcover ISBN: 978-1-4222-3773-1
ebook ISBN: 978-1-4222-8007-2

Cataloging-in-Publication Data is available on file at the Library of Congress.

Developed and Produced by Print Matters Productions, Inc. (www.printmattersinc.com)
Cover and Interior Design by: Bill Madrid, Madrid Design
Composition by Carling Design

Picture credits: 9, Matt_Gibson/iStock; 10, gerenme/iStock; 12, pictore/iStock; 14, minemero/iStock; 15, Brendan Hunter/iStock; 16, MarkSwallow/iStock; 18, Wikimedia Commons; 21, Mike Focus/Shutterstock; 22 (left), Helga Estab/Shutterstock; 22 (right), Tinseltown/Shutterstock; 24, IG_Royal/iStock; 26, CBD/iStock; 27, Ga Fullner/Shutterstock; 29, Horsch/iStock; 30, Natali Brillianata/Shutterstock; 32, Rob Byron/Shutterstock; 34, Sebastian Kaulitzki/Shutterstock; 36, Library of Congress; 37, StepanPopov/Shutterstock; 38, Henrik5000/iStock; 40, Everett Historical/Shutterstock; 41, mtsyri/Shutterstock; 43, Everett Collection/Shutterstock

Cover: agsandres/iStock

CONTENTS

KEY ICONS TO LOOK FOR:

Words to understand: These words with their easy-to-understand definitions will increase the reader's understanding of the text while building vocabulary skills.

Sidebars: This boxed material within the main text allows readers to build knowledge, gain insights, explore possibilities, and broaden their perspectives by weaving together additional information to provide realistic and holistic perspectives.

Educational Videos: Readers can view videos by scanning our QR codes, providing them with additional educational content to supplement the text. Examples include news coverage, moments in history, speeches, iconic sports moments and much more!

Series glossary of key terms: This back-of-the book glossary contains terminology used throughout this series. Words found here increase the reader's ability to read and comprehend higher-level books and articles in this field.

Advice From a Full-Time Professional Investigator of Strange Mysteries

I wish I'd had books like this when I was young. Like other boys and girls, I was intrigued by ghosts, monsters, and other freaky things. I grew up to become a stage magician and private detective, as well as (among other things) a literary and folklore scholar and a forensic-science writer. By 1995, I was using my varied background as the world's only full-time professional investigator of strange mysteries.

As I travel around the world, lured by its enigmas, I avoid both uncritical belief and outright dismissal. I insist mysteries should be *investigated* with the intent of solving them. That requires *critical thinking*, which begins by asking useful questions. I share three such questions here, applied to brief cases from my own files:

Is a particular story really true?

Consider Louisiana's Myrtles Plantation, supposedly haunted by the ghost of a murderous slave, Chloe. We are told that, as revenge against a cruel master, she poisoned three members of his family. Phenomena that ghost hunters attributed to her spirit included a mysteriously swinging door and unexplained banging noises.

The Discovery TV Channel arranged for me to spend a night there alone. I learned from the local historical society that Chloe never existed and her three alleged victims actually died in a yellow fever epidemic. I prowled the house, discovering that the spooky door was simply hung off center, and that banging noises were easily explained by a loose shutter.

Does a claim involve unnecessary assumptions?

In Flatwoods, WV, in 1952, some boys saw a fiery UFO streak across the evening sky and apparently land on a hill. They went looking for it, joined by others. A flashlight soon revealed a tall creature with shining eyes and a face shaped like the ace of spades. Suddenly, it swooped at them with "terrible claws," making a high-pitched hissing sound. The witnesses fled for their lives.

Half a century later, I talked with elderly residents, examined old newspaper accounts, and did other research. I learned the UFO had been a meteor. Descriptions of the creature almost perfectly matched a barn owl—seemingly tall because it had perched on a tree limb. In contrast, numerous incredible assumptions would be required to argue for a flying saucer and an alien being.

Is the proof as great as the claim?

A Canadian woman sometimes exhibited the crucifixion wounds of Jesus—allegedly produced supernaturally. In 2002, I watched blood stream from her hands and feet and from tiny scalp wounds like those from a crown of thorns.

However, because her wounds were already bleeding, they could have been self-inflicted. The lance wound that pierced Jesus' side was absent, and the supposed nail wounds did not pass through the hands and feet, being only on one side of each. Getting a closer look, I saw that one hand wound was only a small slit, not a large puncture wound. Therefore, this extraordinary claim lacked the extraordinary proof required.

These three questions should prove helpful in approaching claims and tales in Freaky Phenomena. I view the progress of science as a continuing series of solved mysteries. Perhaps you too might consider a career as a science detective. You can get started right here.

Joe Nickell
Senior Research Fellow, Committee for Skeptical Inquiry
Amherst, NY

EXPLORING THE MYSTERIES OF THE MIND

The human brain is a vast and mysterious place. Our brains have an estimated 100 billion neurons (nerve cells) firing 5 to 50 times every second. Brains are wired for intelligence, emotion, creativity, and sensation. While scientists have learned a lot about how the brain functions, the gray matter between our ears still holds many secrets. Today, we know that different areas of the brain are responsible for different activities. Even when you're doing nothing, your brain is active—controlling your heart rate, breathing, and other bodily functions.

Many aspects of how the brain works remain unanswered. For instance, how exactly do we store memories? Why are some people smarter than others? Why do we experience emotions? Ten percent of the brain is made up of the neurons or nerve cells that do the actual thinking (the gray matter), and about 90 percent of the brain is constructed of *glia* cells (white matter) that support the neurons. Some say that we have tapped only a small fraction of the brain's potential.

This book looks at some of the more mysterious phenomena related to our consciousness and unconsciousness, along with the science that might explain these phenomena. The conscious brain processes awareness and rational thought. The unconscious mind holds the feelings, thoughts, urges, and memories that are outside of our consciousness. Some scientists and psychoanalysts (followers of Sigmund Freud, the founder of modern psychology) see dreams as a window into the unconscious mind. Dreams have intrigued people since ancient times, and they still do. Why do we sometimes have vivid but unreal dreams? Why do some dreams seem to come true in real life? Did you know that some brains seem to be able to see the future? People have reported having visions predicting future events—from Lincoln foreseeing his assassination to a man haunted by dreams of a plane crash that would eventually come to pass.

The resting unconscious brain can actually make you rise from bed and walk around—all while in a deep sleep. Sleepwalkers have found themselves jumping out of windows, wading into the ocean, and even driving cars.

Have you ever had a feeling that you've experienced something or been somewhere before? It's called *déjà vu* (from the French for "already seen"). Others have a distorted consciousness—some experience seeing and hearing things that are not there (hallucination); others lose memories of their past and think they are someone entirely different from their true selves. The mysteries of the mind are many; read on!

CHAPTER 1

DREAMS

Although you may not remember them, you may have as many as seven dreams in a single night.

Everyone dreams—whether we remember our dreams or not. Since the dawn of humankind, people have been fascinated by these stories that appear before us in our sleep. Ancient Egyptian rulers turned to their dreams to make decisions about how to cure illness, where to construct temples, and when to wage war. During China's Shang Dynasty (1600 to 1046 BCE), court officials had the job of interpreting the dreams of royalty and aristocracy. The ancient Greeks thought that dreams could foretell the future. In the fifth century BCE, the Greek historian Herodotus wrote about King Croesus dreaming that his son died from a spear wound. Although the king did everything to protect his son, one day his son went on a hunt and was accidentally killed by a spear held by the bodyguard assigned to protect him.

Throughout history, leaders have turned to their dreams for guidance. Hannibal, the great leader of Carthage in the second century BCE, said he used his dreams to develop war tactics. Oliver Cromwell, a leader of England in the 17th century, said he dreamed of a gigantic female figure who approached his bed, drew back the curtains, and informed him that he would one day be the "greatest man in England." Adolf Hitler, who would become the German Nazi dictator, had a dream to thank for saving his life as a young soldier in World War I. Sleeping in his trench with his fellow soldiers, he saw them all destroyed by earth and liquid metal. Awakened by this disturbing image, he went for a walk, and during that time, a bomb hit the trench, killing his comrades. On April 4, 1865, President Abraham

Words to Understand

Electroencephalogram (EEG): A test that measures and records the electrical activity of the brain.

Premonition: A strong feeling that something is about to happen, especially something unpleasant.

REM (rapid eye movement): One of the stages of sleep characterized by quick eye movements and paralysis of the muscles. The majority of dreams occur during REM sleep.

Lincoln went to bed and saw visions of people mourning around a corpse in the White House. Lincoln asked a guard who had died. In the dream, the guard said that it was the president— killed by an assassin. Ten days later, John Wilkes Booth would shoot President Lincoln.

President Abraham Lincoln is said to have foreseen his own death in a dream 10 days before he was assassinated.

The Scientific Take: Sifting through Life

According to the National Sleep Foundation, there is no clear explanation as to why we dream. However, Rosalind Cartwright, PhD, professor and chairman in the Department of Psychology at Rush University Medical Center in Chicago, and other researchers say that dreams are essential for incorporating memories, solving problems, and handling emotions.

The ancient Greek philosophers Plato and Aristotle theorized that dreams were a way that people could safely act out unconscious desires, and many psychoanalysts of the 19th and 20th centuries believed in this notion as well. A lot of these scientists, such as Freud, thought that objects and events in dreams might symbolize waking concerns. For instance, being chased in a dream might represent some real-life worry. There are said to be 5,000 dream symbols that can be translated in such a way. Examples include food, which is said to symbolize knowledge; and being naked, which may represent a concern about showing your true self to others.

Scientists have found that our brains are very active during sleep, and that dreams seem to occur during the **REM (rapid-eye movement)** portion of the sleep cycle. Through experiments using an **electroencephalogram (EEG)**, researchers discovered REM and other stages of sleep. During REM sleep, breathing and heart rate quicken, brain activity intensifies, and eye movement increases. In the 1960s, studies showed that the stage of sleep when we dream is vital to mental and emotional health. Patients deprived of this sleep lost concentration, gained weight, were clumsy, felt depressed, and tended to hallucinate. So to sleep deeply and dream is good for our health.

Breakthroughs in Dreamland

Many believe that we work out problems in our sleep, and for some of the world's great scientists, this certainly seems to be the case. Albert Einstein said that his theory of relativity (which explains gravity as a distortion of space and time) started in a dream he had as a teenager. In his sleep, Einstein was riding on a sled that kept going faster and faster until it reached the speed of

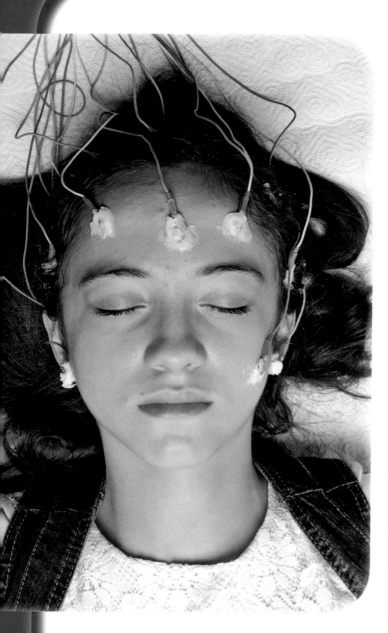

light. At this point, the stars began to distort, and young Einstein saw amazing colors and patterns. He later said that his entire scientific career was related to that dream.

The chemist Friedrich August Kekulé von Stradonitz is said to have come up with the ring-shaped structure of benzene (an industrial chemical used to make plastics, synthetic fibers, detergents, drugs, and pesticides) when dreaming of a snake eating its own tail. A dream of a day at the races led physicist Niels Bohr to come up with the structure of the atom.

Larry Page, one of Google's founders, said the idea for the search engine came to him in a dream he had in college. As he snoozed, Page pictured himself downloading the entire Internet into computers that were lying around. When he awoke, he stayed up a few hours, jotting down his concept. The dream eventually became the search engine Google.

Using an electroencephalogram (EEG) with wires taped to a sleeping person's head, researchers were able to identify the various stages of sleep.

 Learn more about why we dream.

Creativity from Deep Sleep

Some of the most memorable ideas in literature and film were formed when the creators were asleep. Stephanie Meyers said the idea for the *Twilight* series came to her in a dream—she wrote down her night visions word for word and they formed the basis for her hit series of books. The frightening visions of Frankenstein's monster and Dr. Jekyll and Mr. Hyde came to authors Mary Shelley and Robert Louis Stevenson in their dreams. Stephen King is also a believer in the power of dreams. He says that many of his ideas have come in his sleep. "I fell asleep on the plane and dreamt about a woman who held a writer prisoner and killed him, skinned him, fed the remains to her pig, and bound his novel in human skin." The dream fed his imagination as he wrote the novel *Misery*. In the world of music, Paul McCartney says that he awoke from a dream with the tune to "Yes-

One time when film director, producer, and writer James Cameron was sick and feverish in bed, the visions of an apocalyptic future filled his sleeping mind and eventually became the foundation for The Terminator movies.

terday" in his head. Jimi Hendrix, Sting, Keith Richards, and many other musicians have found inspiration while they snoozed.

How do you know you're in a dream? Try to tell the time or read a book. Dream experts say it's impossible to do either in slumber land. But if you easily poke a finger through your hand, you're definitely dreaming!

Seeing the Future

Abraham Lincoln foresaw his own death in a dream, and there have been many other cases where images have come to a person during sleep that seemed to predict events to come. Although mechanisms in the brain might reveal how scientists, artists, and writers have come up with ideas while resting, premonitions are difficult to explain. **Premonitions** are usually feelings that something bad is going to happen. They cause people to feel afraid or uneasy—a sense of dread. Some scientists, such as Persi Diaconis and Frederick Mosteller who wrote the paper "Methods for Studying Coincidences," might say premonitions are just coincidences. But some seem too strange and detailed to to fully understand.

On May 16, 1979, David Booth of Cincinnati awoke from a strange dream: a DC-10 plane flipping over and bursting into flames. He had never had such a dramatic dream before; so this one stuck with him. When he had the same dream the next night, he began to worry. Each night he had the same dream; after the seventh time, he contacted the Federal Aviation Administration. He felt he had to warn them that a disaster might be coming. Officials listened to his tale, but they didn't know what to do with the information. Booth grew more and more panicked as his dreams continued through a 10th day. Then he heard the news: A DC-10 aircraft in Chicago had slipped off the runway, caught fire, and all aboard had been killed.

Mark Twain had a vivid dream about his brother's death. He saw his brother's funeral, his sibling in a metal coffin wearing someone else's suit, and flowers laid on top of him. Strangely, all the details of the dream came true. More recently, a vocalist for the rock group Lynyrd Skynyrd had a dream predicting the airplane crash that would kill many of the band members, and she refused to get on the doomed flight. Many fans thought the band's song "That Smell" was a premonition as well, with lyrics such as "The smell of death surrounds you."

CHAPTER 2

SLEEPWALKING

The Somnambulist, painted in 1871 by John Everett Millais.

Formally known as **somnambulism**, sleepwalking is a relatively uncommon sleep disorder, according to the American Sleep Association. Still, a 2012 study published in the journal *Neurology* found that 3.6 percent of Americans or 8.4 million people had some sort of sleepwalking in the previous year. A somnambulist will walk or perform more complex tasks while asleep.

In most cases, a sleepwalker's eyes are open and glassy, and although they are in a sleep state, they may sit up, look around the room, get out of bed, and walk around. Some perform more complex actions: they go to the bathroom, move furniture, or dress or undress. One four-year-old sleepwalker came into the kitchen and ate a handful of dry cat food—the taste woke him up. One woman awakened with waves crashing around her—she was standing in the ocean a half a mile from her home.

Occasionally, people perform activities in their sleep that are very elaborate. A 12-year-old played piano while in dreamland. Lee Hadwin, a nurse from Wales, has produced amazing works of art in his sleep but can't draw at all when he is awake. American Chef Robert Wood sometimes cooks in his sleep. When she was a teenager, Rachel Ward sleepwalked out her bedroom window in West Sussex, England—she fell one story and survived to tell the tale. Computer expert Ian Armstrong mowed his lawn in London naked—asleep the whole time. Some people report having "sexomnia" or sex while they sleep.

Words to Understand

Insomnia: Persistent sleeplessness or inability to sleep.

Paralysis: An inability to move or act.

Somnambulism: Sleepwalking.

Zolpidem: A popular sedative drug, originally marketed as Ambien, used to treat sleep problems.

Other Sleep Disorders

Here are a few other very rare sleep disorders. Be warned: thinking about them may keep you up at night.

• "Sleeping Beauty syndrome" or Kleine-Levin syndrome sufferers sleep nearly entire days away for several days to weeks at a time. Twenty-year-old Beth Goodier of Manchester, England, who has the condition, says that about every five weeks she is stricken with lengthy 18-hour stretches of sleep, lasting over a period of one to three weeks. During this time, her waking hours are confused and dreamlike.

• Sleep paralysis is a condition of paralysis in which people who are falling asleep or waking up suddenly feel they cannot move, speak, or react. The state is often accompanied by hallucinations, such as seeing demons or hearing a voice of an evil figure.

• Exploding head syndrome sufferers experience hallucinations of extremely loud noises just as they are falling to sleep.

• Fatal familial insomnia steadily causes a lack of sleep to a point of constant insomnia where the person can no longer fall asleep.

The Scientific Take: Signs of a Troubled Mind?

Scientists have characterized sleepwalking as a sleep disorder of arousal. Something stimulates the person to take action as if they are awake. People mistakenly think that sleepwalkers are acting out activities from their dreams, but most sleepwalking does not occur during the REM stage when we dream. It often happens when someone is transitioning from a deep sleep to a lighter stage of sleep. Sleepwalking can be triggered by a lack of sleep, too much drinking, drug use, stress, fever, or a magnesium deficiency. In many cases, it is not a symptom of psychiatric or psychological problems, such as clinical depression or obsessive-compulsive disorder. Most sleepwalkers are children. The American Sleep Association says that 3 to 17 percent of children sleepwalk at some point.

Sleeping Pills and Unconscious Activities

Some people who take the popular sleep aid **zolpidem** find that they wake the next day with mysterious crumbs in their bed or a mess in the kitchen. The Mayo Clinic Sleep Disorder Clinic reports that some who take the sedative-hypnotic drug experience "sleep eating." One woman on zolpidem had incredibly real dreams of cookies all night. When she woke up, she even had the taste of chocolate chips on her lips. When she walked into the kitchen, she was shocked to see the remnants of cookie packages torn open and strewn about. Another woman taking zolpidem woke up in her car—wearing her pajamas, driving, and crying. A nurse who used the drug woke up in her nightshirt after causing a car accident, urinating in the street, and arguing with police. Others have warned about Ambi-texting (for the brand-name Ambien) and the danger of "zzz-mailing" or emailing while asleep. Some scientists say that the drug can put the user in a hypnotic state in which they act out unconscious desires.

The Mayo Clinic Sleep Disorder Clinic reports that some who take the drug zolpidem experience "sleep eating."

Actor Chris Colfer of the TV show Glee says he sleep shops online—an expensive disorder!

Actress Jennifer Aniston has been known to stroll while dozing. She once accidentally set off the security alarm in her home while sleepwalking.

Famous Sleepwalkers

Golfer Sam Torrance injured his hip crashing into a potted plant while sleepwalking. As comedian Mike Birbiglia snoozed, he saw a guided missile heading for him. He threw himself out of a closed window in his hotel room, shattering the glass and ran in a panic—all while asleep. (Birbiglia used his personal stories of sleepwalking to create a hit one-man show called *Sleepwalk with Me*.)

Sleep Talking

About 5 percent of adults will talk in their sleep—and they often can say crazy, nonsensical things. Also called *somniloquy*, the behavior can be brought on by stress, depression, sleep deprivation, day-time drowsiness, alcohol, and fever, according to the National Sleep Foundation. Sleep experts say it can occur during a dream or during a transitionary arousal period when a person is in between a deep sleep and wakefulness.

Dion McGregor was an American songwriter and famed sleep talker. He had bursts of sleep talking that sometimes went on for a few minutes at a stretch. His roommate recorded them and released them as an album. One Englishman living in New York got the nickname of "Sleep Talkin' Man" because of his continuing episodes of sleep talking. His wife kept a record of many of his utterances, including "I haven't put on weight. Your eyes are fat!" "My vision of hell is a lentil casserole." "The bagels have declared independence. The bakery is up in arms! There's a giant flour cloud enveloping everything. Don't trust the macaroons!" Sometimes people sleep-speak in a foreign language—even though they don't know the language.

Comedian Mike Birbiglia talks about his extreme sleepwalking and sleep talking

Killing in Their Sleep?

While people have done some funny things while sleeping, could someone actually kill another person while asleep? Some people believe the answer is yes. In 2005, Jules Lowe on Manchester, England, said he murdered his father while sleepwalking. He was found innocent when a jury decided that he was in an "automaton" state after a heavy drinking session and completely unaware of his actions.

In 1997, Scott Falater, a resident of Phoenix, Arizona, tried to use a similar sleepwalking defense after he was accused of stabbing his wife 44 times—while their children slept in the house. After stabbing her, he dragged his wife to the family pool and held her head under water. He was found guilty after a jury decided that Falater's actions were too complex to have been carried out while asleep.

These cases of sleep-killing are not isolated. Psychiatrist Peter Fenwick reports stories of sleepwalking murderers going back to the year 1600, when a knight stabbed his friend to death. The defense was considered hard to believe then as well. The knight was found guilty.

CHAPTER 3

HALLUCINATIONS

Studies show that almost half of all people will experience a hallucination at some point in their lives.

W hen a person hallucinates, he or she is seeing (lights, beings, objects), hearing (voices, footsteps, music, doors banging), smelling, possibly tasting, or feeling (a crawling sensation on the skin) something that is not actually there. The cause of the sensation may not be real, but to the person who hallucinates, the experience seems as if it is truly happening.

The Scientific Take: A Mental Disturbance

For the most part, hallucinations are caused by some sort of mental disorder—Alzheimer's disease, brain tumor, **epilepsy**, **bipolar disorder**, **psychotic depression**, **PTSD**, delirium, or dementia. About 15 percent of migraine sufferers experience visual aura, which can range from vision loss, to simple hallucinations (typically these are simple shapes and lines). Sometimes they can be fueled by drugs or alcohol. Studies show that about half of all people have a hallucination at some point in their lives.

It's normal for the brain to interpret sights, sounds, feelings, tastes, and smells from external stimuli. But under certain conditions, the senses can be activated without outside stimulus. Mental disorders may flood the brain with confused signals that activate the senses. Interestingly, the brain sometimes compensates for a lack of stimulus. For instance, it's not uncommon for blind people to hallucinate

Words to Understand

Bipolar disorder: A mental condition marked by alternating periods of elation and depression.

Dementia: A chronic mental condition caused by brain disease or injury and characterized by memory disorders, personality changes, and impaired reasoning.

Epilepsy: A neurological problem characterized by sudden and recurring episodes of sensory disturbance, loss of consciousness, or convulsions.

PTSD: Post-traumatic stress disorder is a mental health condition triggered by a terrifying event.

Some historians today believe that Joan of Arc suffered from one of a number of possible neurological or psychiatric conditions, including epilepsy, schizophrenia, migraines, bipolar disorder, or brain lesions.

that they see things, and some people who have lost an arm or a leg hallucinate that it is still there—a condition called *phantom limb syndrome.*

Hearing Voices

Throughout history, people have heard voices from sources that were not there. Some cases may have been caused by a mental condition, stress, or fatigue. The 15th-century French heroine

Joan of Arc heard voices from age 13, telling her to support the French army and fight the English.

Serial killer David Berkowitz, alias Son of Sam, heard voices that tormented him and urged him to kill. He eventually killed six people and wounded seven others; he was certainly mentally ill.

Some voices, however, are harder to explain. Singer Brian Wilson heard voices in his head saying, "I'm going to hurt you, I'm going to kill you." And Brian would reply: "Please don't kill me." During World War II, British prime minister Winston Churchill's "voices" would tell him to "sit here" or "sit there." Churchill was known to suffer from severe depression, which he called his "black dog." Martin Luther King Jr. said that he heard the voice of Jesus promising, "I will be with you."

Research psychologist and TED Talk speaker Eleanor Longden overcame her diagnosis of schizophrenia to earn a master's in psychology and demonstrate that the voices in her head were "a sane reaction to insane circumstances." In college, she began hearing voices saying simple things like "She is opening the door" and "She is leaving the room." Eleanor looked for the source of the voice but could never find it. In time the voices commanded her to do certain illogical things with the promise that she would return to normal life. One time they told her to spill water over a professor's head, and she did. She said at

Lady Gaga has said she hears voices in her head and turns to creativity to get rid of them.

Learn more about hearing voices.

one point she was even tempted to drill a hole in her head to get the voices out. Eleanor grew to learn that her voices were a meaningful response to traumatic life events from her past—she learned that they could be a source of insight to address emotional problems. You can view her TED Talk on hallucinations on YouTube.

"I See Dead People"—Grief Hallucinations

Seeing the face or hearing the voice of one's deceased spouse, siblings, parents, or child may play an important part in the mourning process for some people. Some believe that the "extraordinary experiences" are from actual spirits or ghosts, but some scientists say that seeing loved ones who have passed are hallucinations caused by trauma.

In 2002, a German researcher reported in the journal *Psychopathology* that a woman who had lost her daughter to a heroin overdose repeatedly saw and heard her child saying, "Mama! Mama! It's so cold!" These visions may be part of a grieving process. The famed neurologist Oliver Sacks explained that "… hallucinations can have a positive and comforting role … Seeing the face or hearing the voice of one's deceased spouse, siblings, parents or child … may play an important part in the mourning process." It's possible that these "visitations" help people make sense of death and no longer fear it.

Mass Hallucinations

There have been episodes throughout history where groups of people believe they have seen something (the same thing) that doesn't exist. In 2011, the Monkey Man of New Delhi was terrorizing the city. The Monkey Man stood about four feet tall, and sported a metal cap and steel claws. Rumors spread, and many Delhi residents swore they saw him, but it was likely all in their minds.

Near Newfoundland, for more than a century people have reported seeing a burning ghost

Phantom Limbs

An estimated 6 to 8 out of 10 people who have had an amputation experience a sensation that the limb is still there. They may feel tingling, a prick, numbness, itchiness, tightness, or hot and cold in a part of the body they no longer have. Others feel pain in the limb that is not there. Some report that they feel like they are moving fingers or toes.

One theory is that the severed nerve endings continue to send messages to the brain, which makes a person think that the limb is still there. Touch signals of the entire body are mapped in the brain. When a person loses a limb, the brain is rewiring itself and rearranging sensory information to adjust to the changes in the body. Neuroscientist Vilayanur S. Ramachandran wrote that sometimes amputees feel as though their missing limb is being touched when a person touches another part of their body. When he touched the cheek of a blindfolded man who was missing his left arm, the man said, "Oh my God, you are touching my left thumb!"

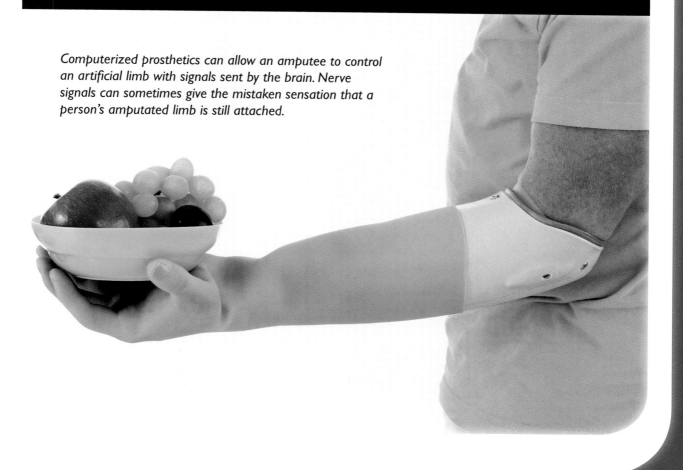

Computerized prosthetics can allow an amputee to control an artificial limb with signals sent by the brain. Nerve signals can sometimes give the mistaken sensation that a person's amputated limb is still attached.

A 2015 photo went viral with people debating the color of the dress.

ship sailing within the Northumberland Strait, which separates Prince Edward Island from Nova Scotia and New Brunswick. Some have even attempted to row out to the fiery ship to save any survivors. Several explanations have been proposed. First, it may simply be a trick of the light combined with shared knowledge of the legend. Another possibility offered by a local botanist is that the illusion was created by the release of methane gas, which rises to the water's surface from underwater coal beds, "playing jack-o'-lantern tricks on unwary humans." Eyewitness accounts like this one, however, make the vision seem very real:

> It was early evening in the fall of the year, November 26, 1965, just turning dark. I was standing near my kitchen window, and when I looked up, I was so startled that I could hardly believe my eyes. There was this ship, on fire and sailing down the Strait. Others looked and saw what I was seeing. As we watched, the ship just seemed to disappear. There was no mistaking it for a real ship.

CHAPTER 4

AMNESIA

A blow to the head can cause amnesia.

Amnesia refers to a general loss of memory, though it is popularly depicted as a loss of memory about one's identity. Jason Bourne (portrayed by actor Matt Damon in the Bourne film series) has amnesia that's wiped out his memory of being a trained assassin. In real life, amnesia doesn't usually involve a loss of identity, but it does happen. Those cases are the ones that make the headlines and are portrayed in films, TV shows, and books. Amnesia isn't just mild forgetfulness—it's forgetting important events in your life, and perhaps not recognizing friends or family.

The Scientific Take: Trauma to the Brain

This memory loss results from some damage to the brain, particularly the parts responsible for memory formation and recollection (the **limbic system**, including the **hippocampus**). A blow to the head can cause amnesia, as well as drug and alcohol use and Alzheimer's, a **degenerative** brain disease. Curiously, investigators have found that those who have trouble remembering the past also have trouble envisioning the future—the two appear to go hand in hand.

Words to Understand

Degenerative: Progressive decline and loss of function in organs and tissues.

Dissociative: Related to a breakdown of mental function that normally operates smoothly, such as memory and consciousness.

Hippocampus: Part of the limbic system involved in forming, storing, and processing memory.

Limbic system: A complex structure of nerves and networks in the brain, responsible for emotions and formation of memories.

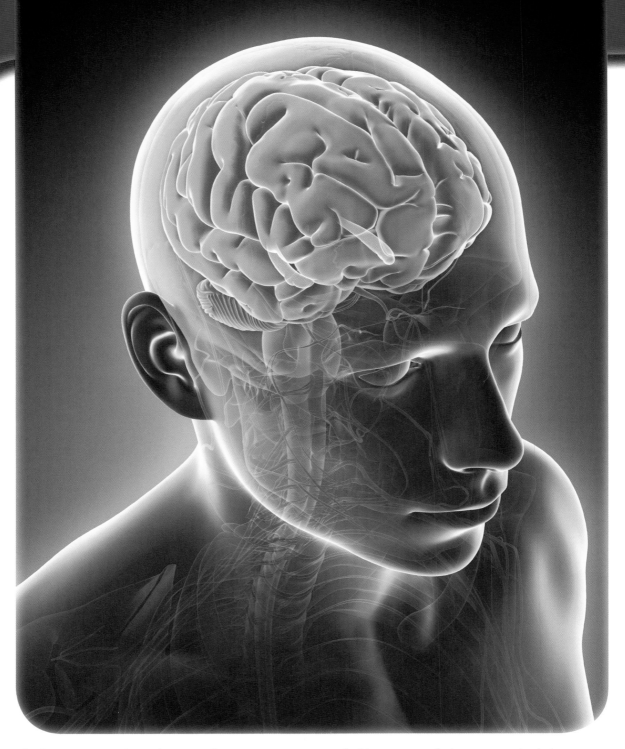

The hippocampus shown here in yellow comprises two interlocking parts and plays a central role in processing memory.

Some common types of amnesia are:

Anterograde amnesia: in which a patient loses short-term memory and cannot remember new information. This is usually caused by trauma, like a whack to the head.

Retrograde amnesia: in which a patient cannot remember events prior to an episode of trauma.

Transient global amnesia: A rare condition in which you are unable to recall recent events, and there may be some loss of older memories as well. The condition is brought on by stress, and even memories of highly eventful days may disappear.

Loss of Self

There are several famous cases where people have totally forgotten who they were and started new lives under new identities. These stories of people waking up with no recognition of who they were generally fit the description of hysterical or dissociative amnesia. With this form of amnesia the person has no idea of who they really are. Sometimes this can be coupled with dissociative identity disorder—the patient switches to an entirely different identity, with no apparent explanation. Some researchers classify this as a type of multiple personality disorder, which is often linked to a severe trauma, such as an accident, natural disaster, or war, for example, or severe emotional, physical, and/or sexual abuse.

Ansel Bourne (the spy action-hero Jason Bourne is named after him), an evangelical preacher, in Greene, RI, had a bout of amnesia that corresponded to a type of dissociative amnesia, although the cause of his problem remains a mystery. He set out on a trip to visit his sister in Providence in March of 1867. Instead of arriving at his destination, he wound up in Norristown, PA, where he opened a store as Albert Brown. About two months later he woke up and wondered where he was. He went to a local physician and told him that he did not know who or where he was. When he found himself in bed that morning in Pennsylvania, he said the shock was like "the report of a pistol." The last thing he remembered was starting out to see his sister. There are several stories like this, and sometimes people with amnesia are accused of being frauds (trying to escape their past)—true amnesia can be difficult to prove.

On February 28, 2013, Californian Michael Boatwright was found unconscious in a Motel 6. When he woke up, he spoke only Swedish, a language he did not speak before. He identified himself as Johan Ek. Boatwright had no memory of his service in Vietnam. He also did not remember his life in a small town in China where he taught English and played tennis frequently. It had been there, at age 60, that he grew depressed and tried to kill himself, taking a mixture of animal tranquilizers and alcohol. After surviving the episode, Boatwright sought a new life in California where he hoped to work as a tennis instructor. After a job fell through, he was found injured in the motel room. Except for his talent coaching tennis, Boatwright's former life was wiped out. No one could explain his new identity or ability to speak Swedish. In time, he abandoned his former life totally and moved permanently to Sweden where he worked as a tennis coach in Uddevalla and told people he was happy. After just over half a year of living in Sweden, Boatwright (now Ek) was found dead in his apartment from an apparent suicide.

Mystery writer Agatha Christie suffered a complete memory lapse.

Similar to Boatwright's story, there have been other people who have had head injuries or gone into comas and come out able to speak a foreign language.

The mystery writer Agatha Christie may be the most famous person to have had amnesia. On December 3,

1926, she disappeared from her home. Her husband apparently was divorcing her, and many speculated that she might have been murdered. On December 14, Christie was found alive and well, registered under the name Teresa Neele at the Swan Hydropathic Hotel in Harrogate. She claimed to have no memory of how she'd ended up there. Some thought the stress from the breakup may have triggered her complete memory lapse.

Learn more about the disruption of memory called amnesia.

Extreme Anterograde Amnesia

Michelle Philpots from England has a unique amnesia story similar to that of Drew Barrymore's character in the movie *50 First Dates*. She suffered head injuries in two accidents and wakes every morning believing it is 1994. All her memories after that point have been erased and short-term memories from each day disappear at night. Similarly, one patient known only as William can remember everything in his life up until 1:40 p.m. on March 14, 2005, and nothing else thereafter.

Naomi Lewis, a British thirty-two-year-old mother, woke up one day thinking she was 15 again, with no memories of the following 17 years

Clive Wearing, a British musician and conductor, had amnesia like in the movie Memento. He had absolutely no short-term memory. His memory span was measured at 20 seconds. Still he had some selective memory—he recognized his wife, could read music, and play piano beautifully.

CHAPTER 5

PRECOGNITION OR SIXTH SENSE

Some scientists have suggested that certain people may be sensitive to electrical fields; their ability to detect a shift in another person's energy could be interpreted as a sixth sense.

Some people are said to have a sixth sense beyond the normal five senses, which allows them to perceive things that are not in what we call the natural realm. A sixth sense is a type of **ESP**. It may be mindreading or the ability to predict the future. It is also called *psychic* or *extrasensory ability*. For some this sixth sense takes the form of **precognition**. They are able to predict or sense things that will happen in the future.

The Scientific Take: Sensing a Shift in Energy?

Although there is no concrete evidence that a sixth sense truly exists, some scientists have suggested that certain people may be sensitive to electrical fields. All living cells have these fields, and a person might be able to detect a shift in someone's energy, which could be interpreted as a sixth sense. Certainly, this does not explain someone's ability to tell the future, but it might explain, for example, sensing that a person is ill when they themselves do not know it.

Other scientific research seems to support the possibility that humans can sense future events. A report on *ABC News* in 2012 looked at research on presentiment (the ability to sense the future) conducted by neuroscientist Julia Mossbridge of Northwestern University in Evanston, IL, and published in *Frontiers in Perception Science*. In an interview, she said that her analysis suggested that if you were

Words to Understand

Clairvoyant: A person who claims to have a supernatural ability to perceive events in the future or beyond normal sensory contact.

ESP: Extrasensory perception, an ability to communicate or understand outside of normal sensory capability, such as in telepathy and clairvoyance.

Precognition: Foreknowledge of an event through some sort of ESP.

Titanic Precognition

Some examples of precognition are so elaborate that they are almost impossible to explain in scientific terms. In 1898, Morgan Robertson wrote a novella titled *Futility, or Wreck of the Titan*. In the story, a fictional ocean liner called the Titan hits an iceberg in the North Atlantic and sinks 400 miles off the coast of Newfoundland—exactly what would happen to the Titanic in 1912.

An 1898 novella seemed to predict the sinking of the Titanic in 1912.

tuned into your body, you might be able to detect these anticipatory changes between 2 and 10 seconds before they happened. For example, suppose you're playing a video game on your computer when you're supposed to be doing your homework and just seconds before your mother comes around a corner, you sense her approach and switch screens and get back to work. According to Mossbridge's research, this type of intuition or presentiment is a real ability.

Premonition

A premonition is a feeling that something is going to happen—usually something bad. On the morning of November 22, 1963, Jackie Kennedy was unnerved by a full-page ad placed in the *Dallas Morning News*. The ad had a black border that looked like a death notice. In 2012, a child at Sandy Hook Elementary left the school two weeks prior to the mass shooting there because of inexplicable panic attacks. Mark Twain was born when Halley's Comet passed by Earth in 1835. He said he would go out with the comet when it passed again in 1910, and—sure enough—he died when the comet came around again. General Ulysses Grant's wife had a feeling he should not go to Ford's Theater on April 15, 1865, the night of the assassination of Abraham Lincoln. They later learned the general had been on a list of those to be killed.

A psychic tells how to develop your **clairvoyant** abilities.

Intuition

Intuition is similar to premonition. It's a gut feeling or hunch. A sense of knowing something without any proof or evidence. In 1936, knobby-kneed and underweight, the racehorse Seabiscuit was a frequent loser. Car salesman Charles S. Howard, however, saw a winner. He had a hunch that the horse was a future champ and bought the animal, despite Seabiscuit's appearance. One night during World War II, Winston Churchill had an uneasy feeling while eating dinner. He told his staff to leave the kitchen. Shortly thereafter, a bomb hit and destroyed the kitchen.

Déjà Vu

Do you feel like you've read this book before? French for "already seen," déjà vu is a sense that you've been somewhere or done something already. Some say they had a dream of a place where they have never been, and then when they visit that location it is exactly as they had dreamed. Some scientists say that the sensation can be explained as a new experience that is similar to an old experience, but the brain is not quite putting all the pieces together. Déjà vu relates to a process in the mind called *cryptomnesia*. The concept of cryptomnesia is that we learn about things, people, places, and then sometimes forget them, yet they are stored in the brain. When you have déjà vu, something may be triggering old forgotten memories to come back.

Clairvoyants and Psychics

A few people throughout history have claimed to be uniquely tuned in to energy that helped them see the future. Jean Dixon and Edgar Cayce may be two of the more recognizable people who made a career out of their psychic ability. Cayce was called the Sleeping Prophet because he saw the future when he was in a meditative state. Cayce correctly predicted the start and

People have always been fascinated with the possibility that they might know their future.

end of two world wars and the deaths of Presidents Franklin Roosevelt and John F. Kennedy. Just 90 minutes before it happened, psychic Tana Hoy foretold the 1995 bombing of the federal office building in Oklahoma City when she was live on the radio. Australian psychic Jeffrey Palmer correctly predicted the devastating tsunami that struck in the Indian Ocean at the end of December in 2004. Harvard professor Diane Hennacy Powell, author of *The ESP Enigma: The Scientific Case for Psychic Phenomena,* believes that everyone possesses psychic ability and some people simply have the genes that allow them to tap into that energy.

Series Glossary

Affliction: Something that causes pain or suffering.

Afterlife: Life after death.

Anthropologist: A professional who studies the origin, development, and behavioral aspects of human beings and their societies, especially primitive societies.

Apparition: A ghost or ghostlike image of a person.

Archaeologist: A person who studies human history and prehistory through the excavation of sites and the analysis of artifacts and other physical remains found.

Automaton: A person who acts in a mechanical, machinelike way as if in trance.

Bipolar disorder: A mental condition marked by alternating periods of elation and depression.

Catatonic: To be in a daze or stupor.

Celestial: Relating to the sky or heavens.

Charlatan: A fraud.

Chronic: Continuing for a long time; used to describe an illness or medical condition generally lasting longer than three months.

Clairvoyant: A person who claims to have a supernatural ability to perceive events in the future or beyond normal sensory contact.

Cognition: The mental action or process of acquiring knowledge and understanding through thought, experience, and the senses.

Déjà vu: A sensation of experiencing something that has happened before when experienced for the first time.

Delirium: A disturbed state of mind characterized by confusion, disordered speech, and hallucinations.

Dementia: A chronic mental condition caused by brain disease or injury and characterized by memory disorders, personality changes, and impaired reasoning.

Dissociative: Related to a breakdown of mental function that normally operates smoothly, such as memory and consciousness. Dissociative identity disorder is a mental Trauma: A deeply distressing or disturbing experience.

Divine: Relating to God or a god.

Ecstatic: A person subject to mystical experiences.

Elation: Great happiness.

Electroencephalogram (EEG): A test that measures and records the electrical activity of the brain.

Endorphins: Hormones secreted within the brain and nervous system that trigger a positive feeling in the body.

ESP (extrasensory perception): An ability to communicate or understand outside of normal sensory capability, such as in telepathy and clairvoyance.

Euphoria: An intense state of happiness; elation.

Hallucinate: To experience a perception of something that seems real but is not actually present.

Immortal: Living forever.

Inhibition: A feeling that makes one self-conscious and unable to act in a relaxed and natural way.

Involuntary: Not subject to a person's control.

Karma: A Buddhist belief that whatever one does comes back—a person's actions can determine his or her reincarnation.

Levitate: To rise in the air by supernatural or magical power.

Malevolent: Evil.

Malignant: Likely to grow and spread in a fast and uncontrolled way that can cause death.

Mayhem: Chaos.

Mesmerize: To hold someone's attention so that he or she notices nothing else.

Mindfulness: A meditation practice for bringing one's attention to the internal and external experiences occurring in the present moment.

Monolith: A giant, single upright block of stone, especially as a monument.

Motivational: Designed to promote a willingness to do or achieve something.

Motor functions: Muscle and nerve acts that produce motion. Fine motor functions include writing and tying shoes; gross motor functions are large movements such as walking and kicking.

Mystics: People who have supernatural knowledge or experiences; they have a supposed insight into spirituality and mysteries transcending ordinary human knowledge.

Necromancy: An ability to summon and control things that are dead.

Neurological: Related to the nervous system or neurology (a branch of medicine concerning diseases and disorders of the nervous system).

Neuroplasticity: The ability of the brain to form and reorganize synaptic connections, especially in response to learning or experience, or following injury.

Neuroscientist: One who studies the nervous system

Neurotransmitters: Chemicals released by nerve fibers that transmit signals across a synapse (the gap between nerve cells).

Occult: Of or relating to secret knowledge of supernatural things.

Olfactory: Relating to the sense of smell.

Out-of-body experience: A sensation of being outside one's body, floating above and observing events, often when unconscious or clinically dead.

Papyrus: A material prepared in ancient Egypt from the pithy stem of a water plant, used to make sheets for writing or painting on, rope, sandals, and boats.

Paralysis: An inability to move or act.

Paranoid: Related to a mental condition involving intense anxious or fearful feelings and thoughts often related to persecution, threat, or conspiracy.

Paranormal: Beyond the realm of the normal; outside of commonplace scientific understanding.

Paraphysical: Not part of the physical word; often used in relation to supernatural occurrences.

Parapsychologist: A person who studies paranormal and psychic phenomena.

Parapsychology: Study of paranormal and psychic phenomena considered inexplicable in the world of traditional psychology.

Phobia: Extreme irrational fear.

Physiologist: A person who studies the workings of living systems.

Precognition: Foreknowledge of an event through some sort of ESP.

Premonition: A strong feeling that something is about to happen, especially something unpleasant.

Pseudoscience: Beliefs or practices that may appear scientific, but have not been proven by any scientific method.

Psychiatric: Related to mental illness or its treatment.

Psychic: Of or relating to the mind; often used to describe mental powers that science cannot explain.

Psychokinesis: The ability to move or manipulate objects using the mind alone.

Psychological: Related to the mental and emotional state of a person.

PTSD: Post-traumatic stress disorder is a mental health condition triggered by a terrifying event.

Repository: A place, receptacle, or structure where things are stored.

Resilient: Able to withstand or recover quickly from difficult conditions.

Resonate: To affect or appeal to someone in a personal or emotional way.

Schizophrenia: A severe mental disorder characterized by an abnormal grasp of reality; symptoms can include hallucinations and delusions.

Skeptic: A person who questions or doubts particular things.

Spectral: Ghostly.

Spiritualism: A religious movement that believes the spirits of the dead can communicate with the living.

Stimulus: Something that causes a reaction.

Subconscious: The part of the mind that we are not aware of but that influences our thoughts, feelings, and behaviors.

Sumerians: An ancient civilization/people (5400–1750 BCE) in the region known as Mesopotamia (modern day Iraq and Kuwait).

Synapse: A junction between two nerve cells.

Synthesize: To combine a number of things into a coherent whole.

Telekinesis: Another term for psychokinesis. The ability to move or manipulate objects using the mind alone.

Telepathy: Communication between people using the mind alone and none of the five senses.

Uncanny: Strange or mysterious.

Further Resources

Websites

International Association for the Study of Dreams: *www.asdreams.org/*
This organization recognizes the value and importance of the study of dreams.

Dream Dictionary: *www.dreamdictionary.org/*
A forum for dream analysis and understanding dream symbols.

Sleep Education: *www.sleepeducation.org/*
A source about all issues regarding sleep, including information on sleep movement disorders.

National Parkinson Foundation: Hallucinations/Delusions: *www.parkinson.org/understanding-parkinsons/non-motor-symptoms/Psychosis*
A section of the website is dedicated to hallucinations and delusions.

NAMI: National Alliance on Mental Illness: *www.nami.org/Learn-More/Mental-Health-Conditions/Dissociative-Disorders*
This association provides information on dissociative disorders, including amnesia.

Movies

Minority Report
Police in the future rely on people with precognition to arrest people before crimes are committed.

Jason Bourne series
Bourne is a spy with amnesia who has to find out his secret past.

Inception
This movie imagines a world where people can break into others' dream worlds and steal or plant ideas.

Further Reading

Birbiglia, Mike. *Sleepwalk with Me and Other Painfully True Stories*. New York: Simon & Schuster, 2012.

Cartwright, Rosalind. *Crisis Dreaming: Using Your Dreams to Solve Problems*. Bloomington, IN: iUniverse, 2000.

Cartwright, Rosalind. *The Twenty-Four Hour Mind: The Role of Sleep and Dreaming in Our Emotional Lives*. Oxford, UK: Oxford University Press, 2012.

Doeden, Matt. *Nostradamus*. North Mankato, MN: Capstone Press, 2007.

Katz, Deborah Lynne. *You Are Psychic: The Art of Clairvoyant Reading & Healing*. Santa Barbara, CA: Living Dreams Press, 2015.

Meck, Su. *I Forgot to Remember: A Memoir of Amnesia*. New York: Simon & Schuster, 2015.

Sacks, Oliver. *Hallucinations*. New York: Vintage, 2013.

Sacks, Oliver. *The Man Who Mistook His Wife for a Hat*. New York: Touchstone Edition/Simon & Schuster, 1998.

About the Author

Don Rauf has written more than 30 nonfiction books, including *Killer Lipstick and Other Spy Gadgets, Simple Rules for Card Games, Psychology of Serial Killers: Historical Serial Killers, The French and Indian War, The Rise and Fall of the Ottoman Empire*, and *George Washington's Farewell Address*. He has contributed to the books *Weird Canada* and *American Inventions*. He lives in Seattle with his wife, Monique, and son, Leo.

Index